Remember your MAGIC!

SONALI CHATURVEDI

BlueRose ONE.com
Stories Matter

First Published in February 2023

ISBN: 978-93-5741-269-8

BLUEROSE PUBLISHERS

www.BlueRoseONE.com

info@bluerosepublishers.com

+91 8882 898 898

Cover Design:

Divya Kardam

Typographic Design:

Divya Kardam

Distributed by: BlueRose, Amazon, Flipkart

ABOUT THE AUTHOR

Sonali Chaturvedi is a mother, inner transformation coach and an activist on a mission to raise human consciousness.

Sonali considers her faith and family to be most important to her. If she isn't spending time reading, coaching and creating contents you can always find her go out on long drive with her husband and cute little boy.

A former IT employee, she always knew she wanted to be an author.The idea for this book came to her while teaching gratitude practice to her 8 year old son.

In this journal she attempts to guide the children on "how to think " and explore the deeper states of mind that regular education ignores.

THIS BOOK BELONGS TO

____

GOAL for it!

Dear Child !

I hope you are feeling exuberant after having this Magical Journal of yours.
It is important for you to take keen interest in how you feel and think rather than just your goals and achievements.

Life is beautiful ! This journal is an attempt to guide you to learn the art of living life to the fullest.

There are three rituals that you can include and plan your daily activities :-

1. AFFIRMATIONS :- There are over 30 affirmations inside this journal.
Purpose :- They make you feel " I AM ENOUGH "

2. GRATITUDE WRITING :- There are over 24 gratitude prompts inside this journal.
Purpose :- They make you feel " I HAVE ENOUGH "

3. GROWTH MINDSET :- There are over 20 growth mindset prompts inside this journal.
Purpose :- They make you feel " I AM ENOUGH BUT I CAN ALWAYS AIM FOR MORE AND I HAVE ENOUGH AND I CAN ALSO ACHIEVE MORE "

Always have an Attitude of Gratitude !

Live life Multidimensional !

love AND light

Rhythmic Return to harmony
Sonali Chaturvedi
Inner Transformation Coach

Try and try again child,
Hit it on the head.
Strike with all your might child,
When the iron's red.
Who they reach the top child,
First must climb the hill.
Standing at the foot child,
Gazing at the sky,
How can you get up child,
If you never try.
So, try and try again child.
Try and try again !

This is me!

age

height

weight

fav toy

fav tv show

fav food

fav teacher

fav subject

hobbies

when I grow up
I want be

my friends are

My Magic

My strengths:

My qualities:

My skills:

Time to reflect on your
favorite moments of the previous year
Capture them here with your
very own time capsule!

Year in Pixels

	J	F	M	A	M	J	J	A	S	O	N	D
1												
2												
3												
4												
5												
6												
7												
8												
9												
10												
11												
12												
13												
14												
15												
16												
17												
18												
19												
20												
21												
22												
23												
24												
25												
26												
27												
28												
29												
30												
31												

PINK - HAPPY

BLUE - SAD

ORANGE - INSPIRED

GREEN - TIRED

BROWN - BORED

RED - ANXIOUS

PURPLE - EXCITING

MIXED FEELING

Colour the boxes with the colour of your choice and track your moods everyday for a year.

Notes:

Periodic Table of

HUMAN EMOTIONS

KEY

LO	JO	AN	SA	FE	DI	SU
love	joy	anger	sadness	fear	disgust	surpurise

LO love											FE fear
GR gratitude	TS trust									NE nervous	SS stress
AD admiration	CO compassion	DI disgust	CT contempt							SM shame	SB submission
TE tenderness	SE serenity	DE desire	OP optimism	AN anger	EV envy	BM bad mood	SA sadness	AB abondanment	LN loneliness	SH shy	TR terror
PR pride	EM empathy	EN enthusiasm	HA happiness	RB rebeillion	RE resentment	HT hate	DS disappointment	WE weariness	BO boredom	DR dread	IN insecurity
SY sympathy	HO hope	EA ease	ST satisfaction	IC incomprehension	AR arrogance	FR frustration	PE pessimism	BL blame	ME melancholia	SU surpurise	SP suspicion
JO joy	EU euphoria	PL pleasure	EC ecstasy	JE jealousy	HS hostility	RA rage	RS resignation	DC discourgement	NO nostalgia	IT interest	CF confusion

My favourite emotions are - ....

3 emotions I feel most often daily - ....

3 emotions I want to feel more in my day - ....

3 emotions I struggle with are - ....

How cool is it
that the divine force
who created mountains,
oceans and galaxies,
looked at YOU and thought
the world needs one of you too.

My travel journal - I travelled from .... to ....

THINGS I DID & THINGS I SAW

PEOPLE I TRAVELLED WITH

FAVOURITE PLACES I VISITED

FOOD I ATE

PLACES I STAYED IN

THINGS I DID NOT LIKE

times when i was sad, irritated, angry, upset

Say yes to new Adventures

FAVOURITE MOMENTS

times when i was amazed, happy, excited, having fun

DRAW SOMETHING FROM MY TRAVEL

5 WORDS TO DESCRIBE THE TRIP

Travel

My travel journal - I travelled from .... to ....

THINGS I DID & THINGS I SAW

PEOPLE I TRAVELLED WITH

PLACES I STAYED IN

FAVOURITE PLACES I VISITED

FOOD I ATE

THINGS I DID NOT LIKE

times when i was sad, irritated, angry, upset

FAVOURITE MOMENTS

times when i was amazed, happy, excited, having fun

DRAW SOMETHING FROM MY TRAVEL

5 WORDS TO DESCRIBE THE TRIP

My travel journal - I travelled from .... to ....

THINGS I DID & THINGS I SAW

PEOPLE I TRAVELLED WITH

FAVOURITE PLACES I VISITED

FOOD I ATE

PLACES I STAYED IN

THINGS I DID NOT LIKE

times when i was sad, irritated, angry, upset

FAVOURITE MOMENTS

times when i was amazed, happy, excited, having fun

DRAW SOMETHING FROM MY TRAVEL

5 WORDS TO DESCRIBE THE TRIP

My 28 day Habit Tracker

Mon	*Tues*	*Wed*	*Thurs*	*Fri*	*Sat*	*Sun*
Lets go!		You can do this!			Keep going!	
You've got this			Don't give up now!			Half way there
	You are doing so well			Look how far you have come		
You are amazing		You are a rockstar				Champion!

Day by day – in every way – I am getting better

Habit that I am building is - ....

My 28 day Habit Tracker

Mon	*Tues*	*Wed*	*Thurs*	*Fri*	*Sat*	*Sun*
Lets go!		Keep going!			You've got this	
	You can do this!		Don't give up now!			Half way there
		You are doing so well			Look how far you have come	
You are amazing			You are a rockstar			Champion!

Your habits decide your future – set good habits

Habit that I am building is - ....

My 28 day Habit Tracker

Mon	*Tues*	*Wed*	*Thurs*	*Fri*	*Sat*	*Sun*
Lets go!		You can do this!			Keep going!	
You've got this			Don't give up now!			Half way there
	You are doing so well			Look how far you have come		
You are amazing		You are a rockstar				Champion!

Day by day - in every way - I am getting better

Habit that I am building is - ....

My 28 day Habit Tracker

Mon	*Tues*	*Wed*	*Thurs*	*Fri*	*Sat*	*Sun*
Lets go!		Keep going!			You've got this	
	You can do this!		Don't give up now!			Half way there
		You are doing so well			Look how far you have come	
You are amazing			You are a rockstar			Champion!

Your habits decide your future - set good habits

Habit that I am building is - ....

Birthday Celebrations

January	February	March
April	May	June
July	August	September
October	November	December

Thankyou very very much!

Mom	Dad	Sibling	Nanny/caretaker
Grand mother	Grand father	Grand mother	Grand father
Teacher	Friend		

3 reasons
why I am grateful for my...

Toys	Books	TV time	Mornings	Snacks

Chocolates	Summer vacation	Play time	Water bottle	Pencil box

School bag

A SIMPLE AND BEAUTIFUL PRAYER!!

* When you wake up, say : God i love you !
* When leaving the house, say : God please come with me !
* When you feel like crying, say : God please hug me !
* When you feel happy, say : God i adore you !
* When you do something difficult, say : God please help me !
* When you make a mistake, say : God please forgive me !
* When you go to sleep, say : Thank you God ! please cover me with your holy mantle.

OTE: YOU CAN TAKE THE NAME OF GOD YOU BELIEVE IN.

Morning affirmations

Evening affirmations

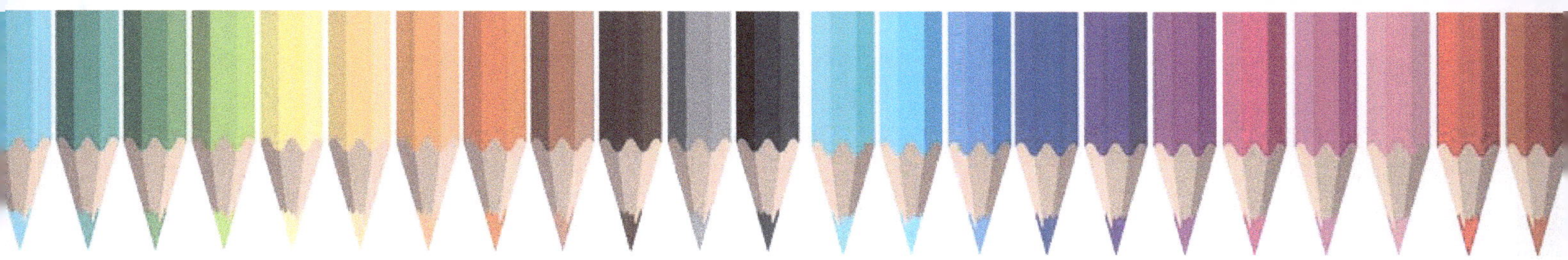

AFFIRMATIONS FOR BACK TO SCHOOL MONDAYS OR AFTER VACATIONS

BACK TO SCHOOL

IT IS OK TO FEEL SCARED, BUT I AM BRAVE.

I LIKE MY FRIENDS AND I CAN MAKE NEW ONES TOO.

I AM READY TO LEARN NEW THINGS.

IT IS OK TO LEARN AT MY OWN PACE.

I BELIEVE IN MYSELF.

I WILL DO MY BEST.

IT IS OK TO MAKE MISTAKES.

I WILL ASK FOR HELP WHEN I NEED IT.

I CAN DO THIS!

I do my best, then I let go of the rest.

I get to choose the kind of day I want.

I get to choose how I feel about my day.

I treat others how I want to be treated.

I see the good in others.

It feels good to be kind and give to others.

I stand up for myself and others.

I take a chance even when I feel scared.

I have the courage to say no, if I need to.

I am brave enough to ask questions, and ask for help.

I can always try again and give my best effort.

I live life to the fullest, and give each day my all.

I say kind thoughts and words to myself.

I listen to my feelings and share them when I need to.

I am grateful for small everyday things.

I am proud of my body and everything it can do.

I can do anything I put my mind to.

I believe in my dreams.

Kindness Matters

Kindness
when others are feeling
hurt, angry, sad scared, upset.

Situation

Mindfulness	Empathy	Compassion
How do I feel about this situation?	How does my friend feel?	What will I do about it?

Situation

Mindfulness	Empathy	Compassion
How do I feel about this situation?	How does my mother feel?	What will I do about it?

Situation

Mindfulness	Empathy	Compassion
How do I feel about this situation?	How does my dad feel?	What will I do about it?

CHARACTER STRENGTHS

CREATIVITY
I think of novel ways to achieve tasks.

CURIOSITY
I am interested in learning and discovering more about the world.

LOVE
I value relationships and being close to people.

FAIRNESS
I treat people equally and without bias.

PRUDENCE
I am careful and cautious when making decisions.

HOPE
I am optimistic, expect the best and believe in good outcomes.

JUDGEMENT
I think carefully about new things and weigh up evidence.

HONESTY
I am a genuine person who speaks the truth and acts responsibly.

KINDNESS
I enjoy helping and doing deeds for others.

FORGIVENESS
I accept and move on from the hurt and shortcomings of others.

HUMILITY
I don't think higher of myself and I allow others to shine.

HUMOR
I enjoy laughter, making jokes and creating happiness.

LOVE OF LEARNING
I enjoy mastering new concepts.

BRAVERY
I accept challenges, am resilient and act on my convictions.

SOCIAL INTELLIGENCE
I am aware of the feelings of others.

SELF-REGULATION
I am disciplined and controlled in my responses.

APPRECIATION OF BEAUTY
I enjoy excellence, beauty and skills in life.

SPIRITUALITY
I believe in a higher purpose and have strong beliefs.

PERSPECTIVE
I provide counsel and help others to see the greater picture.

ZEST
I am enthusiastic and energetic about life.

TEAMWORK
I work well with other people and am a loyal member of group.

LEADERSHIP
I organize, encourage and motivate others to achieve team goals.

GRATITUDE
I am aware and thankful for things that happen.

PERSEVERANCE
I finish what I star overcoming obstacles and challenges.

The more grateful you are

The more beauty you will see

Say everyday...

I am grateful for
my many blessings !

GROWTH MINDSET

QUESTIONS TO ASK YOURSELF

WHAT DID YOU DO TODAY THAT WAS HARD?

WHAT MISTAKE DID YOU MAKE TODAY? WHAT DID YOU LEARN FROM IT?

WHAT WOULD YOU LIKE TO GET BETTER AT?

WHAT HAVE YOU GOTTEN BETTER AT RECENTLY?

WHAT IS SOMETHING YOU ARE CURIOUS ABOUT?

INSTEAD OF		TRY THIS
This is too hard.	→	This may take some time and effort and practice.
I made a mistake.	→	Mistakes help me to learn.
I just can't do this.	→	I haven't yet, but I can.
I will never be that smart.	→	I will learn how to do this.

INSTEAD OF	TRY THIS
I am not good at this.	What am I missing? How can I get better?
I give up!	I will use a different technique, a new way.
I can't make this any better.	I want to improve, I can always improve.
This is good enough.	Is this my best work? I am better than good enough.

INSTEAD OF	TRY THIS
I am awesome at this!	I am on the right track!
She is so smart, I will never be like her.	I am going to learn from her, so that I can try it too.
This plan did not work.	Let's make another plan.
I already know this.	What else can I learn?

LOVE LANGUAGES

5 different ways to show you love someone and 5 different ways to feel loved

1 WORDS OF AFFIRMATION

Compliments, unexpected praise and recognition. Say nice things. Write letters.

2 ACTS OF SERVICE

Doing things for other people that brings them joy. What can you do to make someone happy?

3 PHYSICAL TOUCH

Touch, hugging, holding hands and general physical presence. Cuddling, shaking hands, pat on the back.

4 QUALITY TIME

Spend time with someone, no cell phone or tv while spending time, active listening and making time for loved ones. Listening with your heart.

5 RECEIVING GIFTS

Surprise gifts of thoughtfulness and effort. Small hand made gifts, flowers, favourite snacks, stationary.

MINDFULNESS

Some activities I can do to help me relax include:

Some music I can listen to includes:

Some things I can focus on and think about are:

FAVOURITE BOOK

What is your favourite book and what is it about?

Why do you like the book?

What message or lesson do you learn from the story?

How can you apply the lessons to your life?

ART APPRECIATION

Who created the artwork?

What do you see in the art/drawing?

How does the drawing/art make you feel?

LEARNING IS FUN

What are your favourite subjects?

What is something you have learned in these subjects?

What is something you would like to learn?

What is something you find tricky?

READERS ARE LEADERS !

WORD OF THE WEEK

WORD

PART OF SPEECH

SYNONYM-SIMILAR MEANING

ANTONYM-OPPOSITE MEANING

DEFINITION

USE IN A SENTENCE

MAKE A DRAWING OF THE WORD

READERS ARE LEADERS !

WORD OF THE WEEK

WORD

PART OF SPEECH

SYNONYM-SIMILAR MEANING

ANTONYM-OPPOSITE MEANING

DEFINITION

USE IN A SENTENCE

MAKE A DRAWING OF THE WORD

READERS ARE LEADERS !

WORD OF THE WEEK

WORD

PART OF SPEECH

SYNONYM-SIMILAR MEANING

ANTONYM-OPPOSITE MEANING

DEFINITION

USE IN A SENTENCE

MAKE A DRAWING OF THE WORD

READERS ARE LEADERS !

WORD OF THE WEEK

WORD

PART OF SPEECH

SYNONYM-SIMILAR MEANING

ANTONYM-OPPOSITE MEANING

DEFINITION

USE IN A SENTENCE

MAKE A DRAWING OF THE WORD

SMART GOAL

What is one goal you have for this year?___________________________
Now, fill in answers for each of the SMART goal steps below!

SPECIFIC

Make sure your goal is not vague. Think about *who, what, when where, and why.*

MEASURABLE

How can you measure reaching the goal? What will you use to measure?

ATTAINABLE

Is this goal realistic and possible to reach with effort?

RELEVANT

Why is this goal worth working hard for?

TIMELY

When do you want to achieve this goal?

Goal:

WORK BACKWARDS

Write one goal you have at the top of the page. Now, think about the step you would take right before reaching this goal and write it on the top step. What comes right before that one? Place that below the top step. Keep going! Working backwards is an excellent goal-setting technique!

OBSTACLE

CHALLENGE

Big goals sometimes come with big and small challenges. If you started working on a goal and feel a little stuck, think about what's preventing you from moving forward. Is it distractions, boredom, or is the thing you are working on too hard? Use each block to write one obstacle getting in your way!

BELIEVE IN YOUR OWN POWER

and trust that the magic is within you !

Embrace the beauty of *new* beginnings!

What your parents should say after they yell at you.

STARTING HARD CONVERSATIONS

1. There is something I would like to talk about... is now a good time?

2. I am feeling confused about... would you be willing to help me understand...?

3. I am struggling with something, can I share with you?

4. I was wondering when would be a good time to talk about something that is bothering me?

WISHES AND HOPES

BIG AND SMALL

Use a few words to describe what you hope for in each area in the coming year:

My hopes for the world

My hopes for my school/homeschool

My hopes for myself

My hopes for my community

Create Your Own Map

MY LIFE MAP

How to find FUN, happy moments, friends, and time with my family this year.

Life is a treasure hunt, make your treasure map here!

Cutouts for your map!

SAVINGS

TRACKER

Have a saving goal for the next 18 months? This tracker can help! Write your total saving goal in the star. Then fill in each square with smaller saving goals that you can cross off on your way to the finish!

Stay where
your HEART
feels Alive.
Be patient!
What's
yours will
find you.

JOURNAL CLUB

CERTIFICATE

OF COMPLETION

This Certificate is Presented to

For the enthusiastic participation, and completion of his/her journal. For doing the affirmations almost daily, and developing a growth mindset and an attitude of gratitude. This is a certificate of appreciation

Parent
Director

Another adult
Chairman

9 789357 412698

Printed at Repro India Ltd.